W9-CDN-280

E KAI
Kaiser, Cecily.
On the first night of
Chanukah / written by Cecily
Kaiser ; illustrated by
Brian Schatell.

On the First Night of CHANUKAH

FOUNTAINDALE PUBLIC LIBRARY DISTRICT
300 West Briarcliff Road
Bolingbrook, IL 60440-2894
(630) 759-2102

Written by
Cecily Kaiser

Illustrated by
Brian Schatell

Cartwheel
B·O·O·K·S ®

SCHOLASTIC INC.

New York   Toronto   London   Auckland   Sydney   Mexico City   New Delhi   Hong Kong   Buenos Aires

my brother

me

my baby sister

my mother

my father

my grandp

my grandma

my teache

my auntie

my cousins

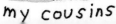

my uncle

my puppy

For Judy Goldblatt, with love
– C.K.

For Nina
– B.S.

No part of this publication may be reproduced, stored in a retrieval system, or transmitted in any form or by any means, electronic, mechanical, photocopying, recording, or otherwise, without written permission of the publisher. For more information regarding permission, write to Scholastic Inc., 557 Broadway, New York, NY 10012.

Text copyright © 2007 by Cecily Kaiser. Illustrations copyright © 2007 by Brian Schatell.

All rights reserved. Published by Scholastic Inc. SCHOLASTIC, CARTWHEEL BOOKS, and associated logos are trademarks and/or registered trademarks of Scholastic Inc.

ISBN 13: 978-0-439-75802-4   ISBN 10: 0-439-75802-5

10 9 8 7 6 5 4 3 2 1   08 09 10 11 12

Printed in the U.S.A.   First printing, October 2007

Library of Congress Cataloging-in-Publication Data

Kaiser, Cecily.
  On the first night of Chanukah / by Cecily Kaiser ; illustrated by Brian Schatell.
    p. cm.
  "Cartwheel books."
  Summary: This version of the popular holiday song celebrates the history and traditions of Chanukah.
  ISBN-13: 978-0-439-75802-4 (pbk.)
  ISBN-10: 0-439-75802-5 (pbk.)
  1. Children's songs, English--United States--Texts. [1.Hanukkah--Songs and music. 2. Songs.] I. Schatell, Brian, ill. II. Title.
PZ8.3.K1244On 2007
782.42--dc22
[E]
                          2007001004

On the first night of Chanukah,
my mother gave to me…

and a menorah burning bright
for all to see!

and a menorah burning bright
for all to see.

3 Stars of David,
2 latkes hot…
and a menorah burning bright
for all to see.

On the fifth night of Chanukah,
my auntie gave to me

4 dreidels spinning,
3 Stars of David,
2 latkes hot…

and a menorah burning bright
for all to see!

On the sixth night of Chanukah,
my uncle gave to me

6 finger puppets,
5 CHOCOLATE GELT!

4 dreidels spinning,
3 Stars of David,
2 latkes hot...

and a menorah burning bright
for all to see!

On the seventh night of Chanukah, my cousins gave to me

7 doughnuts frying,
6 finger puppets,
5 CHOCOLATE GELT!
4 dreidels spinning,
3 Stars of David,
2 latkes hot…

and a menorah burning bright
for all to see!

On the eighth night of Chanukah,
my teacher gave to me
8 special candles,
7 doughnuts frying,
6 finger puppets,

5 CHOCOLATE GELT!
4 dreidels spinning,
3 Stars of David,
2 latkes hot…

and a menorah burning bright
for all to see!